Florida's American Indians through History

Jennifer Prior, Ph.D.

Consultants

Dorothy Levin, M.S.Ed., MBA
St. Lucie County Schools

Vanessa Ann Gunther, Ph.D.
Department of History
Chapman University

Cassandra Slone
Pinellas County Public Schools

Publishing Credits

Rachelle Cracchiolo, M.S.Ed., *Publisher*
Conni Medina, M.A.Ed., *Managing Editor*
Emily R. Smith, M.A.Ed., *Series Developer*
Diana Kenney, M.A.Ed., NBCT, *Content Director*
Courtney Patterson, *Multimedia Designer*

Image Credits: Cover and p.1 United States Capitol/Public Domain; p.3 LOC [LC-USZ62-53566]; p.6 State Archives of Florida/Gunter; pp.7, 9, 12, 29 North Wind Picture Archives; p.8 (top) State Archives of Florida/Bry, (bottom) Marilyn Angel Wynn/Getty Images; p.10 Wikimedia Commons/Public Domain; p.11 Creative Commons File:Crystal River Arch Park TM01.jpg by Ebyabe, used under CC BY-SA 3.0; pp.14-15 Granger, NYC; p.15 LOC [LC-DIG-pga-00467]; pp.16-17 State Archives of Florida/Michael; p.17 Creative Commons File:BISR FL north sign02.jpg by Ebyabe, used under CC BY-SA 3.0; p.18 Creative Commons IMG_0065 by Matthew Hoelscher used under CC BY-SA 2.0; p.19 James P. Blair/Getty Images; p.20 Willard R. Culver/Getty Images; p.21 (top) Patrick Ward/Corbis, (bottom) Rudy Umans/Shutterstock.com; p.22 Jeff Greenberg/UIG; p.23 Creative Commons Miccosukee restaurant, Everglades by Henrik Jagels used under CC BY 2.0; pp.26-27, 32 Willard R. Culver/Getty Images; p.28 Marilyn Angel Wynn/Getty Images; all other images from iStock and/or Shutterstock.

Library of Congress Cataloging-in-Publication Data

Names: Prior, Jennifer Overend, 1963- author.
Title: Florida's American Indians through history / Jennifer Prior, Ph.D.
Description: Huntington Beach, CA : Teacher Created Materials, 2017. |
Includes index. | Audience: Grades 4 to 6.
Identifiers: LCCN 2016014343 (print) | LCCN 2016015178 (ebook) | ISBN
9781493835348 (pbk.) | ISBN 9781433387999 (eBook)
Subjects: LCSH: Indians of North America--Florida--History--Juvenile
literature. | Indians of North America--Florida--Social life and
customs--Juvenile literature.
Classification: LCC E78.F6 P75 2017 (print) | LCC E78.F6 (ebook) | DDC
975.9004/97--dc23
LC record available at https://lccn.loc.gov/2016014343

Teacher Created Materials
5301 Oceanus Drive
Huntington Beach, CA 92649-1030
http://www.tcmpub.com

ISBN 978-1-4938-3534-8

Table of Contents

Tribes of Florida

Two friends walk down a wooden pathway. The path winds for a mile. Along the way, they hear an **osprey's** shrill whistle. They enjoy the shade of cypress trees. They look for hidden wildlife. As they walk, they learn the story of the Seminole Indians. They are at the Seminole Tribe of Florida's Ah-Tah-Thi-Ki Museum. The Seminoles are just one American Indian tribe that has lived in Florida. There are other tribes whose stories should also be told.

Osprey

Ospreys live on every continent except Antarctica. They mostly eat fish, so they have been given the nickname "sea hawks."

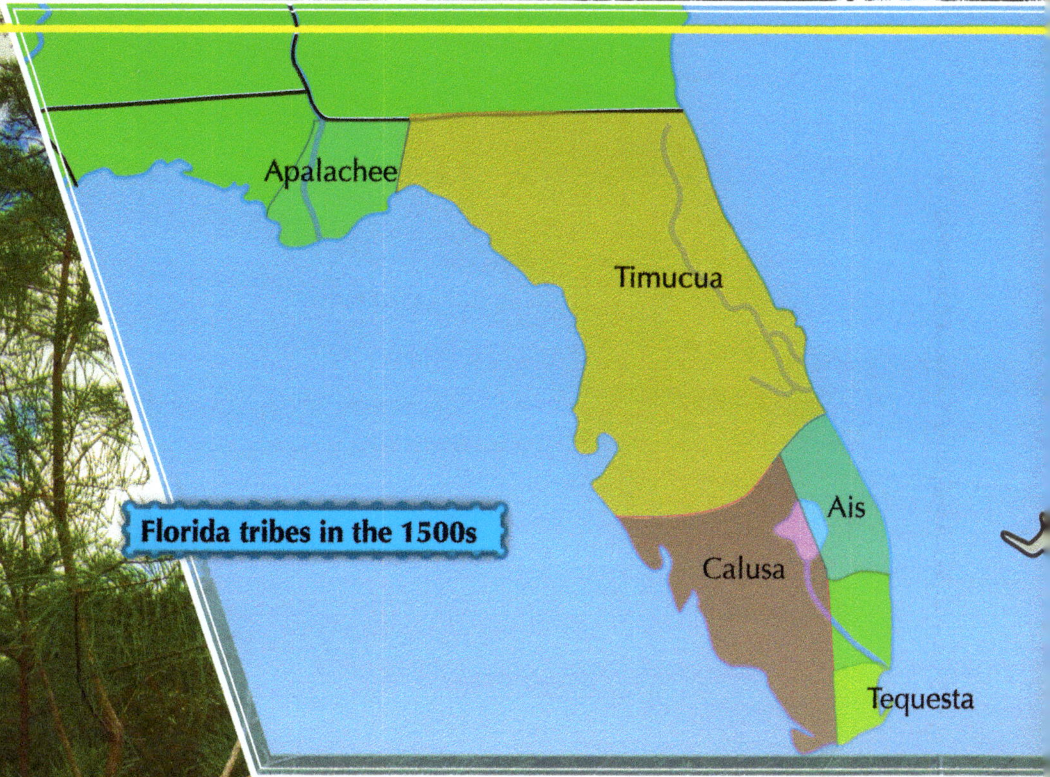

Florida tribes in the 1500s

Many tribes called Florida home long before it was a state. The Calusa (kuh-LOO-suh) lived on the southwest coast. They **descended** from the Paleo-Indians. These ancient people **migrated** to North America during the last Ice Age. The Tequesta lived in South Florida. They were a small and peaceful tribe. The Timucua (tih-MOO-kwah) lived in North Florida. The tribe was made up of smaller groups. Some of their languages reflected a possible Caribbean heritage. The Apalachee of the Northwest were thought of as wealthy and fierce. The Ais (ah-EES) lived on the southeastern coast. They lived along the water in the winter and inland during the other months. These groups had complex **cultures** long before the Spanish arrived. They adapted to their surroundings. Their economies thrived. They each had their own ways of life.

Daily Life

The Calusa Indians were one of the first tribes that explorers encountered. Their name means "fierce people," and they were just that. But life was peaceful within their well-developed towns. They engineered homes on **stilts** and wove roofs from **palmetto** leaves to protect their homes from water. They used waterways to their advantage by digging canals. The canals gave them faster routes for their canoes. Unlike other tribes, they did not farm. Men and boys made fishbone spears to hunt deer. Meanwhile, women and girls collected shellfish. Once the shellfish were eaten, the shells were used as tools, jewelry, and parts of religious **shrines**.

In contrast, the Tequesta Indians lived in small towns. They mainly stayed near water in the Everglades or near **estuaries**. Like the Calusa, the Tequesta ate fish, shellfish, nuts, and berries. Some of their favorites included oysters, catfish, sharks, and jacks. They also hunted deer and wild boar. Objects found at archaeological sites tell us about their daily life. Objects found include tools made of shells. Shark teeth have also been found. Shark teeth were strong enough to carve canoes out of trees. These canoes made travel through wetlands faster than on foot.

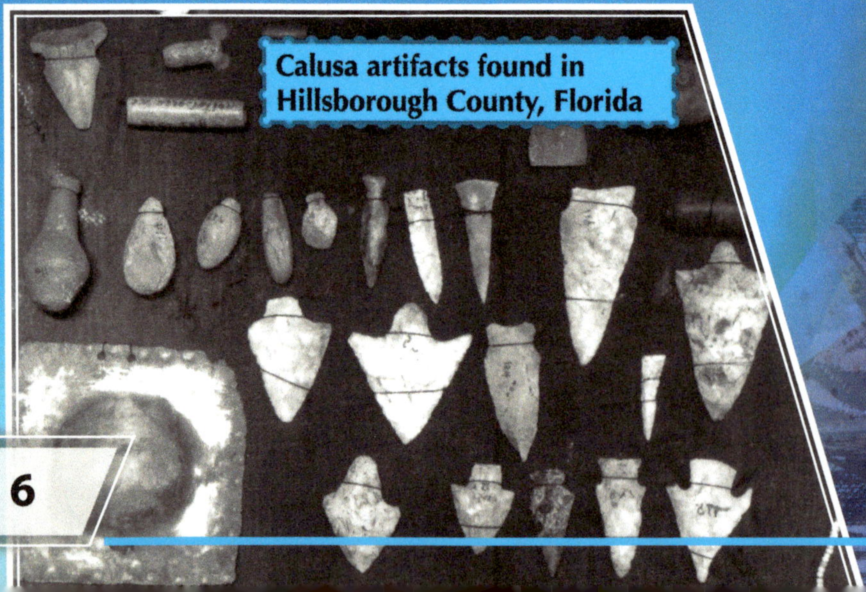

Calusa artifacts found in Hillsborough County, Florida

Beauty of a Palmetto

Many American Indians in Florida wove palmetto leaves to make roofs. The leaves are strong and have a waxy coating. They also have ridges. Ridges help water run off the leaves away from the shelter.

Some Timucua towns looked like this.

The Timucua Indians had more permanent towns. They had small, round homes with palm-thatched roofs. A longhouse with bark walls and the same palm-thatched roof could be found at the center of the town. Sometimes, a 12-foot (3.7-meter) wall of tree trunks surrounded the whole town. Although the Timucua hunted and fished, they also farmed. Their main crops were **maize**, beans, squash, and melon.

Three Sisters

Many American Indian tribes grew beans, corn, and squash. These foods are called the Three Sisters because they help each other grow. Corn stalks let the beans climb. Squash leaves shade the ground. And beans make the soil fertile.

The Apalachee Indians were also farmers. Men prepared fields of maize, beans, and squash. Then, women tended the crops. The fertile soil of the coast produced many crops for the tribe. When farming wasn't enough, men hunted bear and deer while women gathered nuts and berries.

The Ais Indians were not farmers. They were **seminomadic**. They speared fish and collected oysters and clams from the Indian River in the winter. They hunted wild game inland during the summer. In either location, Ais towns consisted of small huts made of wood and sticks. Palm-thatched roofs kept rain out of dwellings.

Timucua Indians farm the land.

Clues about Culture

Although the Ais built burial mounds, people aren't sure whether they were religious. But most of the other tribes were. The Calusa believed in three gods. Their most powerful god controlled the weather, sun, moon, and stars. Clues about the tribe have been found at sites in Florida. The clues include intricately carved masks and shell burial mounds.

The Apalachee were also mound builders. The mounds were a place to praise the sun, moon, and rain. **Artifacts** show that owls and other birds were sacred to the people, too.

Clues about the Tequesta Indians have been found at the Miami Circle. This site may have once been used as a **temple**. Ceremonies may have been held there. Or, it might have helped the tribe track the movement of the sun.

The Timucua also held ceremonies. A **shaman**, or religious leader of the tribe, led rituals for planting and harvesting. The tribe honored leaders who had died.

artifacts found at the Miami Circle

Mounds of Mounds

Many American Indian tribes in Florida built burial mounds for their dead.

Lost Tribes

The Calusa, Tequesta, Timucua, Apalachee, and Ais are now known as "lost tribes." How were they lost? Many of the Calusa died at war with tribes from Georgia and South Carolina. The Timucua and Tequesta also lost many lives in battles against other tribes.

American Indians were killed as countries fought to control Florida, too. Calusa warriors fought to keep the Spanish from raiding their homes. The Calusa and the Spanish fought for many years. They killed each other and enslaved captives.

The Spanish battle American Indians.

Widespread disease was also a major cause of death. The Spanish, French, and British brought diseases, such as smallpox and measles. People in the tribes had not built up **immunities** to fight these new diseases. Many of them died as a result.

American Indians who survived often moved to new places. It's said that the few Calusa left and went to Cuba. The Tequesta and Timucua may have joined the Seminole tribe. Some of the Ais left with the Spanish. The Apalachee moved to Georgia and Alabama. They hid in Louisiana. Some of their **descendants** still live there.

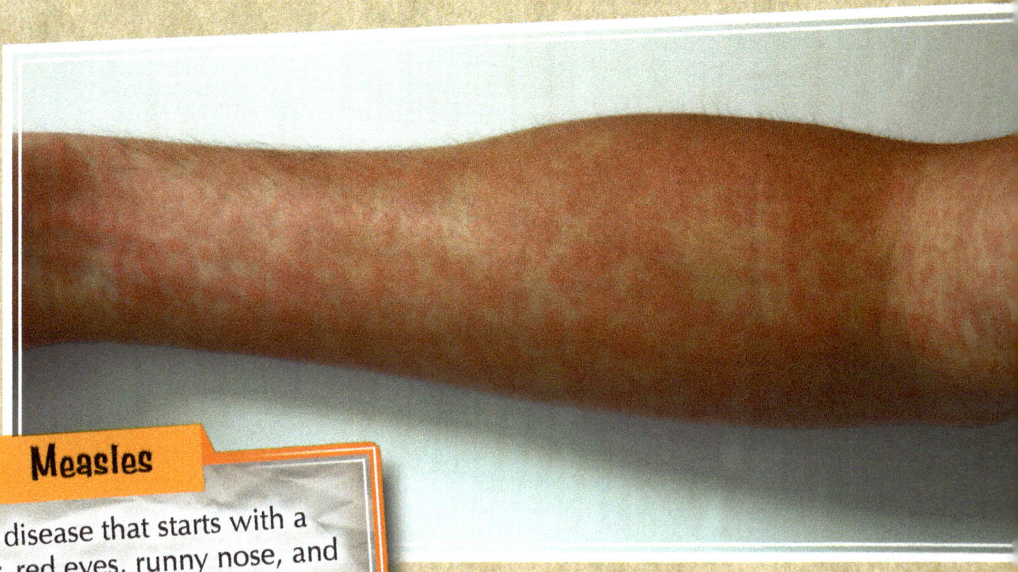

Measles

Measles is a disease that starts with a cough, fever, red eyes, runny nose, and sore throat. Next, a red rash spreads all over the body. This disease is very contagious. It spreads through the air by sneezing and coughing.

The Seminole Wars

The Seminole tribe was not "lost." The tribe's story began in the 1700s. Like the lost tribes, they fought white settlers. They were also attacked by the Creek Indians. The Seminoles moved south to find peace. There, they took in other tribes. They saved Africans hiding from slave owners. This angered white settlers.

Later, the tribe helped the British during the War of 1812. The United States did not want them helping the enemy. In 1817, war broke out between the United States and the tribe. During the First Seminole War, the U.S. Army pushed the tribe farther south.

This engraving depicts an 1830s American perspective of the war with the Seminoles.

In 1830, the Indian Removal Act became law. It said that all tribes would have to move west. But the Seminoles would not leave. A warrior named Osceola led the fight as the Second Seminole War began. Thousands of Seminoles were killed from 1835 to 1842.

In 1855, the Seminoles fought again to stay on their land. Holata Micco, or Billy Bowlegs, led the fight until 1858. He fought bravely and turned down bribes to give up. But eventually, the United States won. Some Seminoles moved west. Some hid in the Everglades. The war was over.

Osceola

It is believed that Osceola was born in Alabama. Although he wasn't a pure-blooded American Indian, he identified himself as such.

Florida Tribes Today

The Seminoles faced many hardships throughout the 20th century. The health of the Everglades dwindled. The United States set aside land for the tribe. But, the tribe found it hard to trust the country. Even so, all was not lost. Seminoles filed land claims. New leaders from the tribe stepped forward.

In 1957, the United States **recognized** the Seminole Tribe of Florida. The Miccosukee (mihk-uh-SOO-kee) Tribe asked for its own distinction in 1962. A third group called the Independent Seminoles is not part of either tribe. Its people don't want the U.S. government in their lives at all.

Today, many people from the first two tribes live on **reservations**. They have councils that govern the people. They keep successful businesses. They educate their children well.

The Seminoles are also trying to restore the health of the Everglades. They want to improve water quality and flood control. They also want to increase the amount of water that can be stored for future use.

Big Cypress Reservation

Welcome To
SEMINOLE TRIBE OF FLORIDA
Brighton Indian Reservation
ESTABLISHED 1957
Johnnie Jones
Board Representative
Andrew J. Bowers, Jr.
Council Representative

Sharing Cultures

Today, the Seminoles and Miccosukee raise their children to value two cultures. They want the cultures of the tribes to be passed to future generations. They also want their children to learn to flourish as part of the U.S. culture.

The tribes share their cultures in other ways, too. Museums help people learn about tribal history. There are annual events, such as the Miccosukee Indian Arts and Crafts **Festival** and Seminole Nation Days. These events give people of each tribe a chance to reconnect and meet new friends. They dance. They play sports, such as stickball and golf. They take part in pageants. They show their arts and crafts. They make and eat food. They listen to storytellers, too.

Miccosukee dancer

Seminoles play stickball at a festival.

A Seminole artist weaves a basket.

Modern-Day Art

The Seminoles are artistic people. So are the Miccosukee. For example, many of them make baskets out of sweetgrass. Sweetgrass is a long grass that is from the local area. It is picked, washed, and dried in the sun. Then, it is sewn with colorful thread. The baskets are very strong due to the palmetto fibers that are often used as the base.

Both tribes are also known for their beadwork and doll making. In the past, beaded necklaces were popular with the women of the tribes. Some women wore up to 12 pounds (5.4 kilograms) at once. The dolls the tribes make portray traditional clothing and hairstyles. Artists make the dolls by wrapping cloth around palmetto fiber husks.

Both tribes are also known for their woodcarvings. The carvings come in many sizes. They may be small figurines. They may be sacred totem poles. Or they may be large canoes.

Math Connection

Seminole patchwork has repeated designs. The designs are created by rotating, reflecting, gliding, and translating shapes.

A Miccosukee artist carves a wooden spoon.

Food

Today, Seminoles and Miccosukee enjoy the same foods as other people in Florida. They shop at grocery stores. They order takeout. There are, however, some recipes that are made for special events. Sofkee is a popular drink. It is made from rice, grits, or oatmeal. In the past, it was made from roasted corn. **Fry bread** is another treat. It is fried dough that is often topped with honey or butter. It is tricky to make but worth the practice. Another popular dish is swamp cabbage. In other parts of the country this dish is called heart of palm. It is prepared by cutting out the cabbage palm and stripping off the outer fronds to reach the heart. It's cooked slowly for about half an hour. The boiled swamp cabbage needs to be stirred to prevent sticking. Most people like to add sugar, salt, or syrup to enhance the flavor.

fry bread

MICCOSUKEE
RESTAURANT
OPEN DAILY: 8:00 AM - 9:00 PM
•HOUSE SPECIALTIES•
GATOR TAIL
BITES
MICCOSUKEE
INDIAN TACO
MICCOSUKEE
FRY BREAD &
PUMPKIN BREAD
BREADED
CATFISH FILLET
FRIED
FROG LEGS

Storytelling

Storytelling is another part of the Seminole and Miccosukee cultures. Legends are stories that are frequently told to each generation. Legends may explain how the world works. They may explain how people should treat each other. For example, a legend might explain how crocodiles got their snouts. Another legend might explain the changing seasons. Legends often communicate what a culture values.

One Seminole legend explains the connection between a croaking frog and rain. In the legend, a rabbit hops up to a sleeping frog. The rabbit can't understand why the frog is content to sleep on such a beautiful day. The frog becomes annoyed. The more the frog tries to sleep, the more the rabbit tries to wake it. The frog decides to get rid of the rabbit by calling the rain. So, the frog starts to croak. Soon, rain falls and the rabbit runs home. The legend explains that a croaking frog signals rain.

Paul Bunyan

What Is a Tall Tale?

A tall tale may seem like a legend because it is fiction. But that's where the similarities end. Legends and tall tales are quite different. Tall tales have heroes with superhuman abilities who solve problems in funny ways.

The Story Goes On

Storytellers weave words into careful shapes. They teach people lessons from the past. They connect people to their cultures. Legends may not always be true accounts of how the world works. But, the stories of Florida's American Indian tribes are true. Each tribe shares its story with the world. Each painting shares emotion. Each event brings joy. Each doll and woodcarving tells of long ago. Each wooden pathway guides guests through the story of the past.

Seminole and Miccosukee people work as teachers and doctors. They work as farmers and bankers. They live in a modern world. They face a modern future. Some of Florida's tribes were lost, but the tribes existing today are strong. Their stories go on.

Children learn about their culture from an elder.

Text It!

Imagine you want to text a friend and tell him or her what you have learned about the American Indian tribes of Florida. What information would you include? What questions might your friend ask? How would you answer the questions? Write your text message. Then, write the possible conversation that would follow.

3G
10:25AM
New Message
To: NoName
Cancel
Send
123
return

Glossary

artifacts—simple objects that were made by humans in the past

cultures—the beliefs and ways of groups of people

descendants—people who are related to groups of people from the past

descended—came from a group of people from the past

estuaries—places where a river flows into the sea

festival—a special event where people celebrate

fry bread—a flat dough that is fried in oil, shortening, or lard

immunities—the body's abilities to fight off infections from diseases

maize—American Indian word for corn

migrated—moved from one country or place to another

osprey—a large hawk

palmetto—low-growing, fan-leaved palms

recognized—accepted something as having legal authority

reservations—land set aside especially for American Indians to live and work

seminomadic—a lifestyle where groups of people move from place to place but have a home at which they cultivate crops

shaman—someone who is believed to be able to cure people who are sick

shrines—places connected with an important person where people go to worship

stilts—posts that are used to hold a building above the ground

temple—a building devoted to worship

Index

Your Turn!

Storytelling

The man in the image above tells children the story about destiny, using a painted wheel of life. Stories that are passed down to each generation teach about a culture's values. What is one story that people tell in your family? Why is the story important? What lessons does the story teach? Write and illustrate a book about that story to share with others.